BUFO

Written by Terra Ciel - Illustrated by L' Étoile

Copyright 2005 © by Terra Ciel

Printed and bound in Hong Kong by Regal Printing

Published by Naturesdance Publishing & Photographix, ™LLC

(NPP, ™LLC)

Evanston, Il 60202 USA

www.naturesdance.com

Illustrated by L' Étoile

Design & Layout by Edward Franco

A letter from Bufo

Dear Children of the World,

Greetings! I love each of you. This is my story. I am delighted to come to you along with my friends so you can read and learn some valuable lessons of tolerance and love. Each of you, like me, is made in a distinct mold and woven lovingly by God´s hands into a special masterpiece, so you are all very special.

Remember, at times in life, you will be wronged and treated badly, but, do not hold a grudge. Smile and continue with being the best you can be. We all make mistakes, and, when you do make a mistake, say you are sorry and do not repeat it. Love each other and always be ready to forgive. Be good to those who are different or unlike you and your friends in any way. They do get hurt when you make fun of them. Do not hurt anyone on purpose. Be kind to all and see how much happiness you get in return. It does not matter if it makes you unpopular when you befriend someone whom no one likes, or, someone who is very different from you.

When you read this book, you will come across many big words. Do not fear them. If you cannot read them; ask your Mama, Papa, Teacher or elder for help. They can help you find the words in a Dictionary. That way you will learn not only the spelling but also the meaning. It will add to your vocabulary (now that is a big word, find out all about it). Remember children, "Those who read are already on their way to greater things in life," and, that is what I wish for each of you.

Learn about my friends and their habitat, learn about the flowers and the trees. Nature gives us so much happiness, protect it. And lastly, I would like you to solve the puzzles at the end of the book. Write to me wherever you are in this world, I would love to hear from you. Enjoy BUFO.

Love,

your friend, BUFO.

BUFO

Once upon a time, there lived a family of frogs by the bridge, near a riverbank. Amongst them was a tiny frog, named Bufo. He appeared very different from all the frogs around him, including his parents. He did not grow like the other frogs did. His color had begun to turn green when he was a tadpole and as soon as he developed into a frog, various colored spots like warts appeared all over his body. The colors of these warts changed from time to time. When he was upset, his body would look like a patchwork quilt. His feet were unlike those of the frogs around him too. All the frogs, big and small, made fun of Bufo. They would never play with him. On the contrary, they would call him terrible names and laugh at him. Poor Bufo was very sad and lonely. He constantly asked his parents this question, *"Why did God make me like this?"* His parents adored their little one. His mother and father were sad for Bufo. They could not get the other little frogs to play with him. And, so it was that Bufo had no friends in his neighborhood.

The other frogs called Bufo a *'chameleon'* because his color and warts constantly changed to various hues. Poor Bufo did not know what a *'chameleon'* is, but he knew they were being mean. He asked his Papa one night what was the meaning of *'chameleon'* and why did the frogs constantly tease him. His Papa explained the meaning and then his Mother said, *"Darling Bufo, do not worry about the names they call you because you are a very special little frog, woven by the loving hands of God into a masterpiece. He made you different because He wanted you to be a very, very special little frog."*

One night as Bufo lay watching the stars light up the night sky like millions of tiny jewels, a tear slowly felt its way down his cheek. His parents were nearby but he made sure they did not see him cry as he quickly wiped away his tear. Suddenly, a shooting star lit up the eastern sky. He watched it as it made its way from east to west across the sky. How he wished he could have a friend, a best friend who would play with him and never make fun of him. His mother, too, had seen the shooting star. She sent a silent prayer to heaven for her son. She wished that he could have a friend. She knew Bufo was a gentle soul and had a beautiful heart. She never understood why the others would not play with her dear son. Although he looked different, he was beautiful to her and to Bufo's Papa. Perhaps, both Bufo and his mother would soon get their dearest wish granted.

Bufo began to remember the events of that afternoon which had made him so sad. Zappy had said, *"I cannot play with you, Bufo. Not now, not ever. My friends say you look strange and you are so different from all of us. You do not look like us. If I were to play with you, then, I would lose all my friends."* Zappy turned and snapped up a passing fly and left Bufo alone, very alone. Bufo turned away, sad and disappointed because he did like Zappy. Zappy had never jeered or made fun of him. He could not understand Zappy's excuse though. Saddened by what Zappy had told him, Bufo went home that evening dejected.

The night faded fast and dawn soon lit up the sky. Bufo set off by himself into the fields nearby, still very sad. He thought he heard a voice call out to him softly, saying, *"Hello there, hello"* and then he heard laughter, it sounded so musical and mysterious. Normally, Bufo would have paid attention to any sound that was unfamiliar, but today, he was so sad that he did not take the time to see who was calling out to him. He hopped along moaning to himself. Bufo returned home that evening, still sad and unhappy. Home was the only place where love abounded. He never felt rejected at home.

"
"Why will no one play with me?"
he wailed.
"

Each day, Bufo was fearful to step out of his house. He knew the moment he went out, all the little frogs would jump behind him and trouble him. They never invited him to play with them. He was so lonely and hopped around by himself. He tried to stay happy despite his loneliness. He did not feel anger towards them, he was just sad that no one played with him; on the contrary, they jeered at him.

One morning, after doing his chores at home, Bufo went off to play by himself not too far from home. He did not know it at the time, but today was going to be a special day for him. He decided to play in the reeds and rushes near the riverbank. Once again, he heard the same soft voice he had heard the day before, this time he stopped and searched the direction from where he had heard it come. The voice seemed to have come from above him. Someone actually called out to him. He waited, and yes! there it was again, two distinct beautiful voices laughing and calling out to him. *"Hello there! look up to the sky. We are up here, we are butterflies,* they giggled, *who are you?"*

Bufo was surprised. He turned around in the direction of the voice and saw the most beautiful creatures with wings, flying around his head. He replied, *"I am Bufo, the frog, what is your name?"* he asked gently. Bufo's parents had taught him well. He was well mannered and friendly. *"I am Flame and this is Indigo. We love to fly just like you love to hop. How are you doing today?"* said Indigo. *"I am well, thank you."* replied Bufo.

"Would you like to play with us?" they chorused. *"I would love that,"* Bufo immediately replied. Indigo and Flame had felt sad for Bufo as they watched him play all alone by the riverbank. They noticed that the other frogs treated him badly because he looked different. They knew that all the other little frogs made fun of him and never played with him. They decided they would play with him. *"We called out to you yesterday too, did you not hear us?"* said Indigo.

Bufo then remembered that someone had called out to him, but he was too sad to take notice. *"I am so sorry,"* he said, then left it at that. Thus was born a unique friendship. Indigo and Flame would fly on either side of Bufo as he hopped amongst the leaves on the ground, trying to keep up with them. They would swoop down and sit on his head and he never even felt them. They all giggled and laughed all the while. Sometimes they would play hide-and-go-seek. Bufo was always breathless trying to catch them as they swerved and dived in and out amongst the bushes. He was so happy that at last he had someone to play with.

Bufo told his Mama and Papa all about Flame and Indigo. They smiled and were happy for their son. Bufo, now happily looked forward to each new day. He knew that either Indigo or Flame would be waiting to play with him. Even though his new friends were unlike him biologically, he loved the fact that they never made fun of him or spitefully call him names. Indigo and Flame were glad to play with Bufo. They were always going to play with little Bufo and make him laugh. Yes! "Laughter is the best medicine."

ne rainy afternoon, as the sun hid behind the clouds, Bufo decided to be daring. He set out to discover the other side of the riverbank. He hopped on to the bridge, at times scared and at times wary. He reached the other side and looked around him, taking in a deep breath. Suddenly, he heard a soft voice close to his ear say, *"Good afternoon stranger, I have never seen you here before!"*

"Hello Stranger, I have never seen you here before!"

Bufo looked up and saw another butterfly. It looked just like Flame and Indigo, only a different color. It had deep stripes across its body. Then, remembering his manners, he said, *"Good afternoon to you too, I am on an adventure today. I live on the other side of the riverbank. What is your name?"*

The butterfly flew upwards. It shyly said, *"I am Striper, what is your name? Would you like to play with me?"* Bufo replied, *"I am Bufo, the frog. Yes, I would love to play with you. You look just like my friends, Flame and Indigo, they also live on the other side of the riverbank."* Striper said, *"I know Flame and Indigo, they are my friends too."*

The rain had stopped, and the sun came out to play. Bufo followed Striper, hopping along further and further into the woods, thoroughly enjoying himself. Indigo and Flame soon joined Striper. Bufo was glad to see them. They flew around Bufo in a circle daring him to follow them and he did. He followed the butterflies oblivious to everything around him. Time stood still as these friends played and enjoyed the day. Bufo suddenly realized that he was much, much further away from home. Yes, he was much farther than he knew. He was so busy trying to hide from his new friends as they played hide-and-go-seek that he lost them, and in the process, he lost his way. He decided to turn back as the sun had almost gone down over the horizon. He knew his parents would be worried. Bufo was scared now. He went left and then right wondering which way to go. Bufo was lost, really lost indeed. The sun had now set and he was very afraid.

eering in the darkness, he saw two red eyes looking at him intently. A mist had risen up and Bufo could hardly see. He was a little scared at first. Then, a voice seemed to boom through the darkness, *"Who are you? What is your name? Are you lost?"* Too many questions all at once! Bufo was surprised, but welcomed the voice. It was not a threatening voice but a kind and pleasant one. Therefore, Bufo, unafraid but timid, replied, *"I am Bufo, I live by the riverbank with my parents. Yes, I am lost. I want to go home. My Mama and Papa must be anxiously searching for me."*

The voice replied, *"I know where the riverbank is, but, it is very far from here. I live near a lotus pond close by. Stay in the pond tonight. When morning comes, you can go home."*

"Who are you? What is your name?"

"I am Bufo, the frog."

"What is your name, and who are you?" Bufo timidly asked. *"I am Bonzy. I am a little white rabbit. They also call me Bunny, or Bunny rabbit. I live in a burrow, under the old maple tree near the Lotus pond."*

Bufo thought awhile, he knew that Bonzy was right. He could never find his way home on this dark misty night. Bonzy sounded genuine and kind. He decided to listen to Bonzy. He replied, *"Bonzy, I am happy to meet you. Thank you for inviting me to stay tonight in the Lotus pond. I think it is a good idea. I will go home in the morning."*

Bonzy said, *"Bufo, follow me closely so that you do not get lost again."* Soon they came to the lotus pond. Bufo was so excited that he took one big leap and landed in the pond. He landed safely on a lily pad, not afraid anymore. They said good night to one another and Bonzy hopped into his burrow close by. Bonzy felt sad for Bufo so far away from his home and friends.

The next morning Bonzy awoke very early. The sun was just peeping over the horizon. The sky was aglow with beautiful hues of orange, red, pink and purple. He rushed to the edge of the pond to check whether Bufo was doing well. He called out loudly, *"Bufo, where are you?"*

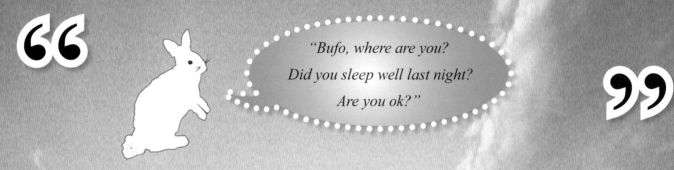

"Bufo, where are you?
Did you sleep well last night?
Are you ok?"

"Did you sleep well last night? Are you ok?" Bonzy had a strange habit of asking many questions at the same time. It was his style. Bufo was just glad to hear Bonzy's cheery voice early morning. He happily answered, *"Good morning, Bonzy. Yes, I did have a nice sleep. These lily pads are very soft. I have never slept on one before."*

"Please do not go home today. Let me show you my world. Stay here and be my friend." Bonzy begged Bufo. Bufo was surprised. No one had ever wanted to play with him before, leave alone ask him to stay and be a friend! Yes, except for Indigo, Striper and Flame. Bufo now had something to think about seriously. Bonzy's offer was extremely tempting. Bufo also liked the lotus pond.

Bonzy was hungry and needed to eat. Bonzy asked Bufo if he would like to go with him in search of food. Bufo said he would be glad to. They both took off together on a food adventure. Bufo made sure to stay close to Bonzy as he did not want to get lost again. Suddenly, he saw someone familiar flying towards him. *"Could it be?"* he wondered. Yes, there they were, both Indigo and Flame, his friends. They seemed to be troubled. Bufo was glad to see them. They called out to him, *"Bufo, we are glad we found you. What happened to you? We looked all over for you last evening. Your Mama and Papa are also worried about you."* Bufo's parents searched for him everywhere and were anxious for some news of their dear son. Bufo told Indigo and Flame, *"I was lost yesterday, but Bonzy here, found me and invited me to stay at the Lotus pond. Please tell them that I am well and not to worry. I will be home tomorrow."* Both Indigo and Flame promised to deliver the message to his parents. They were overjoyed to see Bufo. They told him that they missed him and Bufo in turn, invited them to stay at the Lotus pond.

Bufo had never had so much fun before. It was the first day away from the riverbank. He was truly enjoying himself, thanks to Bonzy. Time passed quickly and one day led to another. Each evening, Bufo would decide to stay one more night at the Lotus pond. He would tell Bonzy about his decision and Bonzy would become very happy. Bufo seemed to have made a very special *'friend'* in Bonzy.

Bufo had stayed on at the pond much longer than a few days now. He loved to play and hop around on the lily pads in the pond. The pond sat at the farthest end of a great big piece of land behind a big old House. There were lovely flowers of every hue around the pond. No other frogs lived in the pond. He was extremely happy in this new world. The pond was also home to two beautiful fishes. One was gold and the other blue. They both became Bufo's friends. They loved Bufo, the friendly frog. When Bufo was in the pond, they danced around him and played with him.

One fine morning, bright and early, Bufo got up and hopped along to the entrance of Bonzy's burrow. He called out to Bonzy, *"Bonzy, are you still asleep? I have been thinking about my home. I have a secret to tell you."*

Bonzy shouted out rather quickly from within his burrow, *"Which home?"*

Bufo looked at him confused and replied, *"My home, the one by the riverbank."*

"Oh!" said Bonzy disappointedly. His heart began to sink for he knew in his heart that Bufo missed his Mama and Papa and had wanted to go back home. *"I know I want to see Mama and Papa, but......"* stammered Bufo. *"But, but what, Bufo?"* questioned Bonzy quizzically. *"But, for now, I have decided to make the lotus pond my home."* blurted out Bufo.

"There, I said it," thought Bufo to himself excitedly. Then he took one giant leap on to the lily pad in the lotus pond. Bonzy could not believe his ears, he jumped out of his burrow, shouting loudly, *"Yippee! Bufo, I am so glad that you are going to stay."* Bufo became very happy to hear what Bonzy said to him. He knew in his little heart that he had made the right choice to stay at the Lotus Pond. He silently thanked God for saving him through Bonzy, the night he was lost.

"Yippee! Bufo, I am so glad you are going to stay."

Now that he decided to make the lotus pond his home, he was going to enjoy every minute of the day with his new friends. He was becoming very popular in and around the pond. There were many who had made the pond their home, settling in and around it. They would often tell him interesting stories. Bufo was a good listener. At times, he would hop into Bonzy's burrow and tell Bonzy about his new friends and life in the pond. At other times, Bonzy just sat beside the pond as Bufo sat on a lotus pad and they chit chatted about everything around them.

Bonzy had many tales to tell Bufo because he traveled a great deal while looking for his food. He spent a lot of time in the carrot and lettuce patch near the big old House. There was also a strawberry garden nearby, which he loved to visit. Bonzy seemed so brave and he was not afraid of anything. Bufo loved Bonzy because he not only had saved his life the night that he was lost, but, he was also a good friend. Neither did Bonzy nor anyone in the *'pond family'* make fun of Bufo. Bonzy had warned Bufo not to stray too far away alone because it was dangerous. He watched out for little Bufo and Bufo was in awe of Bonzy. He did not want anything bad to happen to his new friend. Bufo listened to Bonzy and never ventured out alone.

Bufo was kind to everyone. He knew what it was to be disliked. He now had made many friends. One such friend was lovely Queenie. She had an orange colored head with green and turquoise colored feathers. She liked Bufo and loved to sit and sing to him. Queenie lived in the old Maple tree close to the pond. Danny was a beautiful yellow Finch. He trilled melodiously all day long, flitting from tree to tree. At times, he would swoop down to say *'hello'* to Bufo and hop on to a lily pad near him. Danny had his home in the Crab-apple tree near the pond. Then, there was Dizzy, the enchanting hummingbird. She zipped from flower to flower, drinking nectar and spreading cheer all around. She could hover above a flower without touching it while her wings *'zipped'* back and forth at an extraordinary pace, making everyone dizzy. Dizzy's wings flapped seventy times per second. That is how she got her name.

Long Legs occasionally visited the pond. Danny did not like Long Legs or *'LL'* as they all called him. Danny did, however, smile at him whenever he visited the pond. Danny never sang in the presence of LL, nobody knew why, and no one asked Danny the reason either. LL mostly kept to himself. He seemed very proud as he stood amongst the reeds and bulrushes watching everyone with amusement. Bufo liked LL but he was scared of his long beak and stayed far from him. Bufo told Bonzy about the new friends he had made: Queenie, Dizzy, Danny, LL and the gold and blue fish. Bonzy was very happy that Bufo was no longer sad.

At last, one day, Bufo decided to tell Bonzy why he had never wanted to go back to the riverbank. He told Bonzy all about how the other frogs treated him and how they made fun of him and said horrible things about him. He said that they would not have him as their friend because he did not look like them. Bufo also told Bonzy that he missed his parents but he was happier here in the pond. He knew that his parents would understand. He said that he would definitely go back one day to see them. He thanked Bonzy for bringing him to the Lotus pond.

Bonzy felt sad for Bufo. He said, *"Bufo, it really does not matter how you look, you have a beautiful heart and you are kind, that is why we all love you. You can stay forever here at the pond if you like. We all would love you to stay here amongst us. No one will ever make fun of you again."* Bufo was glad to hear what Bonzy said to him. He knew that Bonzy sincerely wanted him to stay. Bonzy on the other hand was glad to see Bufo happy. Bufo was a good friend to all.

Bufo loved his new home very much. There were white and yellow lotuses in the pond on whose leaves he loved to sit and daydream. Pansies grew at one end of the pond. Large roses grew in the bushes around the pond. There were also bulrushes along the edge of the pond. Close by, there was a beautiful Jasmine bush and a flowering crab-apple tree where Danny lived. The perfume of the jasmine flowers filled the night air. A Magnolia tree grew on the edge of the pond at one end. This was indeed paradise. Bufo felt very lucky that Bonzy found him that night or he might have perished. Bufo would do anything for Bonzy.

One morning, there was a great deal of commotion around the pond. There were new comers in their midst. It was a handsome pair of Blue Birds. Queenie named them the *'BBs'*. They had begun making their home in the giant Elm tree close by. Mrs. BB was picking out the best twigs and hay to line her nest. Queenie was excited, chattering constantly. She called out to Bufo and Bonzy and introduced them to the BBs and to all the *'pond family'*. They all gave the Blue Birds a hearty welcome. The BBs soon became a part of the *'growing pond family'*.

One early morning, Bufo and Bonzy decided to go out on a long hop together. The sun was just rising. Streaks of white clouds scattered the gorgeous sky, sailing across ever so slowly. The warmth of the sun and the gentle east wind made them very happy and they were thoroughly enjoying the morning.

In the distant, they could hear Danny's melodious trill as he flit from tree to tree. Yes, it was a perfect morning for everyone. Bonzy and Bufo were busy talking, laughing and chasing each other around. Bonzy asked, *"Would you like to go to my favorite place, the Carrot patch?"* *"Is it far from here?"* asked Bufo. *"No,"* said Bonzy, *"but, it is close to the big House."*

The carrot patch was right behind the big House. Bonzy and Bufo were busy hopping about the shrubs, mostly hidden from view. Bonzy stopped to nibble at a small carrot, which had broken off and fallen to the ground. *"Yum, Yum,"* he said, as he chomped on his carrot.

Bufo was busy hopping around trying to catch a large bug as it flew around his head. He had become adept at catching these insects. *"Wow! this is really tasty,"* thought Bufo. They were busy enjoying their little picnic, quite content in their new friendship. Bonzy reminded Bufo once more, saying, *"Be sure and stay close to me because the 'Quackers' (geese) are always around the big House, and they are dangerous."* Bufo nodded looking up at Bonzy. This was turning out to be a great day for both of them as they played together.

Suddenly, Bufo heard a noise. He thought it was Bonzy hopping around the carrot patch. Bufo was engrossed in trying to ensnare a large bug. Then, again, he heard it, ever so slightly closer to himself, *Thump! Thump!* Bonzy had heard it too and dismissed it thinking that Bufo was hopping around trying to catch insects. Then this time the *'Thump'* was right behind Bonzy. Bonzy thought that

Bufo had jumped up behind him and he turned around. Bufo was scared and looking up at something fearfully. Bonzy looked at Bufo. Then, very slowly, he took a quick peek in the direction that Bufo was looking. He still had his carrot in his mouth. He saw a man who was crouching over him. In his hand, he had a net. Bonzy was scared and did not know where to hide. He quickly looked around for a way to escape, there were none. Bonzy was trying to think fast, but he froze and before one could say *'jack rabbit'* a net fell on him and trapped him. Bufo nervously jumped over the man's big shoes and disappeared around a boulder. He strained his neck to watch his friend struggle in the net, he was now sick to his stomach. In a matter of seconds, his best friend was a prisoner. He knew that Bonzy was in danger. Bufo was helpless and so was his friend.

The man had a green hat with a wide green brim on his head and a multi-colored cloak around his shoulders. He had a patch over one eye and a long moustache. Bufo wondered if Bonzy knew who he was! The man held Bonzy by his two ears. *"Ouch,"* thought Bufo, *"That must hurt."* The man carried Bonzy into the big House. Bufo followed, jumping cautiously behind him.
Suddenly, he saw the *'Quackers'* waddling towards him, quacking away. He remembered what his friend Bonzy had told him, and he took off shouting, *"Help, Help,"* with the geese after him.

"Help! Help!" cried, Bufo.

ufo had managed to dodge the *'Quackers'*. He darted to the other side and hopped off in a hurry to his home. He was terribly unhappy now. He was so alone. Bufo was scared too. He kept thinking about Bonzy and praying that he would be all right. He did not know what they would do to Bonzy in the big House.

He decided to go back to the pond for a little while. He hoped that someone there could help him. He noticed that LL was visiting the pond. Everyone knew LL was very intelligent. Most of the pond was scared of him but they were never rude to him. They thought that LL was very proud because he preferred to be by himself.

Bufo went over and told him about Bonzy. He told LL that Bonzy was caught in a net by a man and taken to the big House. He asked LL if he thought his friend would be safe. LL looked at him. He thought a while and then he said, with a twinkle in his eye and a wink at no one in particular, *"Your friend, my dear, is going to be cooked. He will be served on a golden platter for supper tonight in the big House. Yes, they just love to eat bunnies."* Then, he lifted his neck and let out a great big laugh. Bufo gasped, then, looking at him angrily, he said, *"LL, it is no wonder no one talks to you. You cannot be a friend to anyone. I thought you were my friend. Friends do not talk about friends like that nor do they wish evil on their friends."*

Bufo was sick. His legs felt faint now and he stopped to take a deep breath. *"Oh dear! It will be terrible if this man harms my friend,"* thought Bufo. He wrung his hands. He must do something to save Bonzy, his best and most precious friend in the world. Bufo then angrily turned to LL and said, *"LL, you are extremely unkind and rude, you should have offered to help me instead. How would you like it if you were caught in a net and none of your friends could help you or save you? I am never going to talk to you again."* Bufo knew he did not mean it but LL's remarks did hurt him.

Long Legs was shocked. Bufo never talked to him like that. He had something serious to ponder. Bufo, in the meanwhile, left him and jumped into the pond. Whenever Bufo got upset, his body would change colors, and, this was one such time. His body looked like a patchwork quilt. Bufo was extremely upset about Bonzy's kidnapping. He was going to pray and think, and, perhaps talk with his friends, the fishes. Exhausted and worried, Bufo said a little prayer that his mother had taught him, *"Dear God, please help me be strong,"* and added, *"Help me save my dear friend's life, keep Bonzy safe."* Bufo now felt strong and he knew in his heart that God was going to help him save his friend. He just did not know how.

Bufo began to tell the fishes about Bonzy's misfortune. The fishes listened patiently to Bufo because they loved him. They said, *"Bufo, we are so sorry about your friend. We wish that we could help you. You know we cannot leave this pond or we will surely die, but, we will pray that Bonzy is safe and will come back to us."* Bufo thanked his friends and told them that he understood their predicament. Bufo was going to save his friend, come what may. Suddenly, he heard a familiar voice from above him. Bufo looked up and saw Queenie. She called out to him and then flew down and sat on a branch not far from him. She asked, *"Bufo, why are you so upset today?"* Bufo told her all about the big man who had captured Bonzy. He described the man and his attire. Queenie then told Bufo that the man was a Magician. Bufo asked Queenie, *"What is a Magician?"* Queenie replied, *"A Magician makes things disappear."* Then, Bufo was afraid. I hope the man did not make Bonzy disappear. *"What would happen if Bonzy could not be found?"* He shuddered to think.

Queenie closed her eyes, reminiscing, and was upset. Her feathers automatically stood up near her neck and made her look very imperial when she was angry. When she heard about Bonzy's capture, she turned to Bufo and said, *"I know what it is like to be a prisoner. I used to be the Magician's prop. I escaped one day and flew away from my captors. I now enjoy my freedom. I will not be a prisoner again."* Then she continued, *"Do not worry, Bufo, I will help you find your friend. Perhaps, I can fly around the big House and look in to see if I can spot Bonzy."*

Then Bufo said, *"Thank you Queenie for helping me. Yes, please fly to the big House and see if you can spot Bonzy anywhere and let me know."*

So Queenie, spreading her wings, took off towards the big House. She circled it a couple of times, looking in through the windows. She disappeared from sight for quite a while and then she returned, very disappointed. Queenie looked at Bufo as he sat helplessly and very unhappy on the lotus leaf in the pond. *"How could she break this news to him?"* she wondered. She knew he would be sad. Then Queenie flew down to the edge of the pond and said, *"Bufo, I did fly around the house, I am so sorry but I cannot see Bonzy at all."*

Bufo was heartbroken. He really did not know what to do. One thing he knew for sure, no matter what happens, he would search for his friend and bring him back. That was a promise he made to himself. He thanked Queenie for trying to help. He told Queenie that he was going into the big House. He also told Queenie to let all his friends know so that they can try to help him find Bonzy. Queenie knew the House very well. She warned him about Sheba, the dog and Pluto, the cat who lived in the house. She flew down and told the BBs, Danny and Dizzy about Bonzy's plight and how Bufo was very sad. Mrs. BB flew down to the pond and called out kindly to Bufo, saying, *"Bufo, we are so sorry to hear about Bonzy. We will help you search for your friend. Do not worry, you will find him soon."*

Bufo felt a lot better by now. He was glad for his friends who loved him very much and he loved them in return. His friends offered him support. His spirits began to soar. Bufo prayed that all would be well with Bonzy. He dared not risk going out this late because he did not wish to get lost again. The gold and blue fish stayed close cheering him on and telling him that he would find his friend. Bufo sat down and closed his eyes to rest so that he could be strong enough and able to help his friend the next day.

There, it was again, streaking across the sky from east to west, a great big *'shooting star'*. Bufo smiled, knowing in his heart that all would be well with Bonzy. He felt that this was a sign for him not to worry anymore.

Early next morning, Bufo proceeded to the big House very cautiously. Bufo knew his mission. He looked around and then headed for the main doorway. From the corner of his eye, he saw a fat white goose come dashing towards him. He took one long leap and landed close to the main doorway, hiding in a large potted plant. The goose stood near the flower pot glancing in from time to time. Bufo shivered peeking

through the leaves. Time passed on and the goose stood her ground. Then, losing her patience, she stuck her beak here and there in the pot and not finding Bufo, headed off angrily in another direction.

"I am sure she is upset because she lost a tasty meal today," thought Bufo. He let out a sigh of relief. He waited with baited breath. He did not know if the big man had come out of his house or not but he decided to hide in the potted plant for a while until the coast was clear. It was a good place to hide for the time being. He had to get into the house at any cost. Then, his patience was rewarded, the big man came out empty-handed, and shut the door quickly behind him. Bufo was not quick enough to sneak into the door. It had begun to drizzle. The air was cold and wet and a mist hung over the trees and the House. Everything looked ghostly. Bufo knew that it was the perfect time to try to get into the House. He must find another way. He saw the Quackers as they made their way towards the big House. Bufo did not want to meet them so he went behind the House, away from the geese. He leapt onto a tall plant near the window and looked back to see if he was being followed. He then jumped onto the window ledge and looked into the window, straining his neck. However, sadly, he saw nothing, nothing at all. He also heard nothing and this made him very sad and upset. He refused to give up. Bufo did not despair. After all, he was on a mission to save his friend. He then jumped on to another window ledge and from there he hopped on to the fire escape stopping every now and then to make sure he was not in any danger. He waited, breathing heavily, tired a bit and thinking constantly.

He slowly made his way to just under a third window ledge. Fortunately, there was an old box near it. He jumped up and from there onto the window. Voila! He saw that the window was a tad open to let in the fresh air. Bufo attempted to squeeze himself through the window. *"I have got to slim down a bit,"* grumbled Bufo. *"If only he could make it through the bars on the window,"* he thought, breathing heavily. He waited a while. Then, he tried again with all of his might and one last tight squeeze got him in successfully. Bufo sighed! He saw a large ball in the room, close to the window, behind the curtain. He looked right and then left and not seeing anyone inside, he took one big leap and managed to land on it perfectly. He rubbed his sides that were bruised by the iron bars on the windows. *"Ouch, it hurts,"* he gasped. He had just made himself comfortable on the large ball behind the curtain, when he heard a footstep come softly into the room. He hid and balanced himself carefully peering through its gossamer folds. He saw a little girl with pretty curls. She had her head down and seemed to be talking to someone. Bufo kept hiding. He could now see the little girl holding something in her hand.

She was saying, *"Bessie, today is my Birthday. My friends are coming to my party. I know Papa has a surprise for me. I wonder what it is! I hope it is not another doll. I already have three dolls. I have Priscilla, you, and then, there is Missy. I just love you Bessie, you are my favorite doll, because Mama*

16

gave you to me. I also love Sheba and Pluto. Papa and Mama gave them to me last Birthday. Oh Bessie, I do miss Mama so much." Sophie looked at her Mother's portrait above the mantel and tears filled her eyes. She touched her Mama's photo and kissed it. Bufo felt sorry for Sophie.

ufo wondered about the little girl's Mama. Did she also get lost like him? He began to think about his Mama and he missed her too. He shook himself from daydreaming. He must concentrate on saving his friend while not being caught. He was visiting a House for the first time. He must carefully note everything around him. He did not want to forget how he got in here, in case he had to scoot in a hurry. *"My word! I will have so much to tell everyone at the pond,"* thought Bufo. He started to daydream once more almost losing his balance. Bufo recovered quickly and reminded himself, *"Focus, Bufo."*

Bufo wondered if he was not too late to save Bonzy. *"What if they ate him already?"* Then shaking himself, he said softly, *"No, I am going to be positive, I am definitely going to find my friend today."*

Bufo was upset with LL for telling him that the people in the big House must have eaten Bonzy by now. The thought kept coming to his mind repeatedly. Bufo promised himself that he would not rest until he found Bonzy.

The little girl picked up the balloons in her hand and left the room. Bufo followed her ever so quietly. This was indeed a very different world from his. He looked carefully at the stairs and wondered about them. He was in awe of them. He then saw the little girl walk down the stairs, one-step at a time. Her Papa was calling out to her. The little girl began hurriedly descending the stairs. Bufo came down a few too, and hid just behind a column. He waited for her to go down. He followed her with his eyes as he saw her go down rung after rung. It looked like there was no end to the stairs. Her Papa kept calling out to her. The little girl ran down faster. Bufo kept his eyes on her. He quietly went down a few rungs as well and waited patiently. She was standing on the last but one rung. Bufo was so far up, hidden from view. Her father stood at the foot of the stairs and called out to her once again, *"Sophie darling, jump and I will hold you."* Sophie was hesitant at first. Her Papa cajoled her and Sophie jumped safely into his arms. *"Happy Birthday, darling,"* said her Papa and planted a big kiss on both of her cheeks. Her Papa then said, *"Would you like to see your Birthday gift now?"* Sophie replied excitedly, *"Oh yes, Oh yes, Papa, I would like that very much,"* skipping along as she called out, *"Pluto, Sheba, come, see my new present."* No one moved or came to her. She held on to her Papa's hand and skipped along with him to see her surprise.

Bufo peeped in between the railings of the staircase. He tried looking around, but saw no sign of Bonzy. Far down instead, he saw two animals, much larger than him. This must be Sheba and Pluto, he thought. One was sitting behind a plant and the other was close by. They both were very beautiful creatures. Bufo had never seen such creatures before but he remembered what Queenie had told him, so he made sure to stay away from them.

A door slammed somewhere in the distant and soon, the maid walked into the room. She looked at them and called out to Sheba. She did not move. Pluto, the cat came running in and rubbing himself against her legs, began purring loudly. Bufo was more cautious because now there was another person in the home. The dog was sleeping despite the noise around her. Near her nose was a large bone. *"I guess she will not be eating me tonight,"* thought Bufo. The dog kept pricking up her ears now and then in her sleep. Bufo had to stay very silent. No matter how fast he could leap, he was sure they would be faster. He did not want to take unnecessary chances. He knew he must avoid both of them. Queenie had told him just that, Bufo remembered. He decided to wait a little longer. He waited patiently for a chance to make his way down the rest of the stairs. Yes, Bufo did have a lot of patience.

The little girl's Father held on to her hand and disappeared around the corner. *"Oh dear, I am going to lose them now."* Bufo thought anxiously. Somehow, he believed that as long as he could see the little girl, he would not be lost. Bufo also noticed that the little girl's Papa looked different from the day before. He looked rather kind and smiled often at his little girl.

Bufo decided it was time to take the next step. Then, heart beating wildly, he descended the awesome stairs. He turned the corner, groaned as the second set of stairs came into view. He jumped four stairs at a time very quietly but rather hurriedly. He cautiously peered through the railings of the stairs. He saw neither the man nor the little girl. He panicked. Fortunately, he did not see the dog, cat or the maid. Perhaps they had taken off after the little girl. Bufo sighed once more.

Bufo took another quick look around. At first, he thought he would just slide down the banister for it would be faster. However, on second thought, he did not want to cause a stir. He looked down once more, then to the left and the right making sure that the coast was clear. Yes, it was. He did not have to worry about being eaten up alive. He hurriedly started jumping down, flinging himself a few rungs at a time and then he stopped. Not far from the ground now, he heard the little girl, *'Ah! a familiar voice.'* He listened carefully. *"Yes, that was indeed the little girl's excited voice,"* knew Bufo. *"Oh Papa, Papa, show me my gift now, I am so excited,"* said the little girl jumping up and down.

That means they were closer than Bufo thought. Bufo waited on the stairs, scared to continue. He did not yet know the direction they actually were. He also did not know where the dog and the cat were. Bufo's heart was beating like a kettledrum against his chest. He did not want to become anybody's meal. His color had begun to change once more. All seemed totally quiet and eerie. Then, he heard the little girl shout out excitedly. Bufo did not know why. He hopped down a few more rungs and turned towards the direction of the voice. Just then, he heard the little girl say, *"Oh, Papa, give me the Bunny, can I hold the Bunny for just a little while?"* Bufo closed his eyes. *"Where had he heard the word 'bunny' before?"* he wondered. Bufo tried to remember. He closed his eyes, thinking again, *"Where have I heard that word before?"* Then, in a flash it came back to him, he remembered that Bonzy had told him the very first night they met that people also called him a *'bunny.'* He would never ever forget that night. That fateful night Bonzy had saved Bufo and God willing, today, Bufo would return the favor. He then remembered that LL had called Bonzy a *'bunny'* too. Bufo perked up.

Again, he heard Sophie say, *"Oh Papa, this is truly the best gift. A live bunny rabbit, my very own Bunny, can I play with him now?"* He remembered what Bonzy had told him the first night they met, saying, *"I am a white rabbit, they also call me Bunny."* Bufo froze at first. Then, he was extremely happy to know that his friend was still alive. Throwing caution to the winds, with great big leaps, he jumped down almost fainting with anxiety. He slowly went around the corner, the voices grew louder and, he saw them. Bufo quickly hid under the table. He could see nothing now. He was scared to move, knowing that the little girl's pets were around. *"Darling, you can play with the Bunny for as long as you like, but, be sure to put him back in the cage when you are tired. Sophie, make sure you lock the cage."* *"Yes, yes, Papa,"* the little girl replied, jumping up and down with happiness. Her Father excused himself saying, *"Sophie, honey, I must go out now and I will be back shortly, enjoy your new friend. Remember again, do not forget to lock the cage."* Sophie replied, *"No Papa, I promise not to forget to lock the cage."* Her Father planted a great big kiss on Sophie's forehead and left the room with Sheba, close on his heels. Pluto seemed unhappy as he watched the little girl hold the Bunny in her arms.

"Meow, I thought that I was your favorite! Meow...Meow"

20

Pluto seemed hurt and kept meowing constantly. Pluto watched anxiously from his perch on the table. Bufo waited with baited breath wondering about it all. Soon Pluto, bored and upset, jumped off the table and ran out of the room. Bufo sighed in relief. He now had only to keep an eye on the little girl as she held and played with her new friend. She kissed Bonzy many times and was extremely happy with her gift. She kept telling Bonzy, *"You are the best gift that I have ever received."* Bufo was overcome with happiness, for here was his friend, not far from him and looking well.

Sophie's father was going to shop for his little girl's party that evening. Bufo knew this was his opportunity. He did feel sad for the little girl but he wanted to save his friend. He once again thought about his Mama and Papa and sent a prayer their way. Now, he could concentrate on Bonzy and figure out how he was going to save him. He quietly jumped up on a chair in the corner from where he had a great view.

There was a pretty cage on another table. There were some green leaves spread inside the cage and a bowl of water. He knew that the cage was now Bonzy's new home. He then thought about Queenie's story. He was glad that Queenie was safe. Bufo knew that his friend had spent the night in the cage. He also knew that somehow that would be the last night his friend would be in the cage.

The little girl held on to her Birthday gift tenderly. She kissed Bonzy numerous times and petted him. She held him close to her. Bufo bided his time. Bufo was a patient frog. He would have to wait until he had an opportunity to talk to Bonzy. He also watched out for Pluto and Sheba just in case they came back. Bonzy made no sound. He seemed to be enjoying all the attention. He even had a pink bow around his neck. *"I am sure that Bonzy must dislike that,"* thought Bufo. He knew Bonzy loved his freedom. After playing for quite a while with her new pet, the little girl seemed tired. She began to yawn and rub her eyes. She kissed her Bunny and said, *"Dear little Bunny, I love you very much, do not be sad. I will*

come back and get you later when my friends arrive. I am going to show them what a beautiful present my Papa gave me for my birthday." She then hugged him once more and kissed him, put her dearest *'Birthday present'* in the cage and locked it. She left the room with Bessie in her arms.

Bonzy was all curled up and looked so sad. Perhaps he was thinking that no one at the pond would miss him. He might also be thinking that Bufo had forgotten him. Nevertheless, here was Bufo trying desperately to free his best friend. This is my chance, thought Bufo. It is now or never. He waited until all was quiet. Then he called out to his friend softly, *"Bonzy."* Bonzy's ears shot up. He looked around. The voice sounded familiar. And, again he heard his name called out, *"Bonzy, Bonzy,"* Bufo whispered, *"I have come to take you home."*

Immediately, he heard his friend excitedly say, *"Bufo, where are you? I always knew in my heart that you would come to save me."* Bufo said, *"Shhhhh! be silent, someone will come in. I am sure you noticed that there is also a dog and a cat around and we do not want to play hide-and-go-seek with them. I can see you in the cage."*

Then, Bonzy sat up in excitement, nose smack against the bar of the cage. Bonzy was glad his friend did not leave him to die. His friend had come to save him. Bonzy was delighted. He jumped up and down in the cage not heeding the warning from Bufo. He just wanted to go home. Bufo jumped onto another chair close by, and then, onto the table, where the cage stood. He was glad to see that his dear friend was unharmed. He told him how sorry he was that he could not come earlier. Bonzy heard nothing, he just wanted to leave the big House.

Bonzy told Bufo to hurry up and open up his cage. Bufo tried several times and was unable to. He was tired and time was running out. Bufo felt helpless, and then he remembered how Bonzy had saved his life one night. He said a little prayer and began once more to tackle the lock, this time he stuck his toe under the lock and gave it a little push. Lo and behold! The lock slid aside. Bufo was able to open the door of the cage. Free at last. Bonzy hesitated awhile, *"Come on now, surely you do not like your new digs that much?"* teased Bufo.

Bonzy jumped out of the cage without a moment's hesitation. Bufo warned Bonzy again about the cat and the dog. Bufo was scared that Bonzy would not be quiet and either the pets or a human would catch them. Bonzy was brimming with happiness and could not contain his joy at being free and being able to leave the cage and the big House. On his mind was one thing, and one thing alone, 'FREEDOM!'

They stealthily climbed up the first flight of stairs. It was getting dark and the sun was ready to sleep. They must get out of the house now. Bufo and Bonzy stopped repeatedly to make sure that no one was following them. After making sure that no one was around, they swiftly went up the second set of stairs. Bufo directed Bonzy to go further down the hallway because he now knew that the window he came into at first, belonged to the little girl's room. They found another window opened at the end of the hallway. Bonzy asked Bufo to hop on to his back, and to hold on tightly. Bufo did, Bonzy took a flying leap off the ground, cleared the window and soon they were outside. They both wondered to themselves, *"Were they out of danger yet?"* They dared not look behind them. Just then, they heard someone call out to them. They hesitated and prayed that they would make it safely down to

the lower roof. *"Hang on, Bufo, I am going to take one more jump,"* said Bonzy. Then he took a great big jump. They heard familiar voices coming towards them. They saw Queenie and Danny fly down over them flapping their wings. They called out to Bufo, *"Bufo, you are safe, you are safe. Quick, jump down and come to the pond. Dizzy, the BBs and the fishes are all waiting for you."* Bufo, perched on Bonzy's back shouted out, *"Thank you, Queenie and Danny."*

Then Bufo hopped off Bonzy's back and they hastened to descend the lower roof. They jumped together, 'plop, plop,' into the strawberry garden just behind the big House. This time there would be no surprises as they were extremely careful. In addition, their feathered friends were watching over them to warn them. Bonzy did not even stop to eat the lovely strawberries on the ground. They made their way to the lotus pond hurriedly. On the way, Bonzy thanked Bufo repeatedly. Bufo assured him that he would have done the same for him if he were captured instead. Bufo was so happy that he was able to save his friend's life.

Danny and Dizzy flew down and chattered incessantly with Bufo and Bonzy. The pond family was present and they all cheered Bufo. Queenie began singing, *"Bufo is a hero, Bufo is a hero today."* Danny decided this was the perfect time to trill and there was music in the air. Queenie was very happy that Bufo had found his friend. She knew what it was to be a prisoner.

ow that all was well, Queenie decided to check out the big House because she knew the little girl must be sad once more. So, off she flew to the big House. She sat quietly on the ledge of the window, looking in and watched the proceedings below. Mr. Horn Rim sat wisely watching Queenie from his hideout. Something was surely up. He knew Queenie would never come back to the big House.

He was going to sit just out of Queenie's view to watch her. Queenie knew Horn Rim quite well. Horn Rim had tried once to trouble her and she retaliated with such fury that he left her alone. Now, they were nice to one another. When Bufo came to live at the pond, Queenie had warned Horn Rim never to touch her friend or else he would be sorry. Most of the pond family never knew Horn Rim because he came out at night only when all the others were asleep. Horn Rim was a beautiful snow owl who had come to the Lotus pond much before Queenie. He had a broken wing and that made his search for food quite tedious. He stayed close to his home in the giant Oak tree at all times.

eanwhile, in the big House, the little girl was fast asleep upstairs in her bed, before her birthday party. Her dolls lay all around her as she slept. Sophie's Papa was happy that she loved her birthday gift. He wanted her to be happy because she missed her mother so much.

The maid came in just before the party and put up streamers, balloons and colored lights all around the house. The house looked beautiful. The maid then went upstairs and awoke Sophie. She helped Sophie to bathe and get ready for her party. Sophie dressed up. She had on a beautiful green dress with a red border, her hair looked pretty around her face. She went downstairs to see if her Papa had come home. She was excited to see all the decorations. Pluto came running in, Sophie played awhile with him and then she sat down to wait for her Papa and her friends. She did not want to go and see her Bunny yet, because, later on, she wanted to surprise her friends with her Birthday gift. Her Aunt, Uncle and Cousins came in with gifts. Soon her friends began arriving and there was much chatter amongst the friends. Everyone had brought Sophie a birthday gift. She thanked each one. She put the gifts on the table beside her. Her father came down and greeted everyone. He took Sophie's hand in his and went to the dining table. Kristin pulled Sophie aside and whispered, *"Sophie, what did you get for your Birthday? Tell me please, I will not tell anyone."* Sophie replied, *"I will tell all of you together, after we eat. No, I will show all of you the best Birthday gift any girl could have."* She then smiled and closed her eyes, thinking how happy she was with her newfound friend.

Samantha

Kristen

Shelly

The ceiling was festooned with beautiful colored balloons that seemed to be hanging in space. There was a big gorgeous cake on a platter in the middle of the table with a Bunny sitting on top of it. Sophie clapped her hands in delight. She smiled a mysterious smile because the Bunny looked so real, just like the one her Papa had given her for her Birthday earlier today. The maid brought in the birthday gifts and laid them on a table close by. The table was decorated beautifully in red and green, Sophie's favorite colors.

Sophie's aunt stepped into the living room and sat at the piano while everyone surrounded Sophie and sang to her the *'Birthday'* song. They all then went back to the dining table. Sophie blew out all her candles in one big breath, and cut her cake. Her family and friends sat down to eat. Everyone was happy. Sophie's friends were anxious to know what she had got for her Birthday from her Papa. They could not contain their curiosity. Kirsten once more asked, *"Sophie, what did your Papa give you for your Birthday?"* *"Yes, please tell us Sophie,"* chimed in Shelly and Samantha. Sophie looked at them and smiled mysteriously. She then said, *"I will show you my Birthday gift after we eat."*

Sophie was deliriously happy today. This was the best day of her life. Her Papa was home and so were her Uncle, Aunt and Cousins plus her three best friends. She sadly thought about her Mama now and then. This was her first Birthday without her Mama.

Sophie loved to share her toys with her friends. She knew they would love her Birthday present. She was going to let each of them hold her little Bunny before they left. She closed her eyes and thought about all the games she would play with her Bunny. *"Sophie, wake up, are you tired?"* said her Papa. *"No Papa,"* she smiled a great big smile and said, *"I am thinking about someone."*

Sheba sat around hoping to get some cake and goodies from anyone who would give her. She hardly ever left Sophie's side except when someone gave her a bite to eat. Sheba was a beautiful dog, she just loved the attention she received. Her friends began to eat hurriedly because they were anxious to see Sophie's birthday gift. As soon as they had eaten, Sophie ran up the stairs to bring down her gift.

Then, suddenly, she called out hysterically to her Papa, *"Papa, Oh! Papa, please come up,"* shouted Sophie. She was sobbing and screaming hysterically at the same time. Her Papa ran up the stairs two rungs at a time wondering what had made his little girl cry out like that. He was followed closely by her Aunt Cathryn and the maid. Sophie clung to her Papa, shaking his hand and crying, *"Papa, Papa, she screamed, my Bunny has gone. See Papa, see, the cage is empty."* Indeed, Bonzy, the Bunny had left the premises. Her Papa was sad to see his little Sophie crying and so distraught on this, her special day. He said, *"Honey, do not cry."* He kissed her and held her in his arms. *"I will look for your Bunny, he must be somewhere around, I hope that Sheba or Pluto did not hurt him."*

Sophie's Papa did not know that Bonzy was unharmed and back in his burrow. He took Sophie once more in his arms and kissed her. He promised her that he would get her another Bunny if her Bunny were lost. Sophie was so upset that she did not want to come down to her friends. Her Father insisted that she be the perfect hostess and come down and tell her friends what had happened to her gift. Her Father reminded her that even though her mother was not alive, she would have wanted her to do just that. Sophie always obeyed her parents. She came down to the living room where her friends were. They were anxiously waiting for Sophie. They wondered what had made their dear friend so upset. Samantha was even crying. Sophie told them about her gift and how the Bunny was now gone. They felt for her deeply as she sobbed out her story. Sophie was utterly heart broken. She did not want to celebrate anymore.

Her friends hugged her and told her not to worry. They said, *"Sophie, we are sure that your Papa will find your Bunny soon."* It was getting late and her friends had to go home soon. Sophie thanked them for their gifts with tears in her eyes. Her friends were sad for her. They hugged her again and said, *"Sophie, we love you, please do not cry, we are sure your Papa will find your Bunny soon."* Then off they went to their homes.

Queenie had heard and seen it all. She flew back to her nest. The next day she warned Bufo, *"Please, do be very careful when you go out again, Sophie's Papa has promised to find Sophie another Bunny rabbit soon."* Queenie then whispered something into Bufo's ear and Bufo nodded, smiling a secret smile. Bonzy had overheard everything that Queenie said about the little girl, except the whisper. A shiver went up Bonzy's spine. He thought how he surely would have had to live in the cage for the rest of his life if Bufo did not save him. He thanked God for Bufo. Bufo and Bonzy thanked Queenie, Danny, Dizzy and the BBs who had helped them. Bufo also did not forget to thank the fishes for making him feel better when he was so sad earlier. They swam around Bufo in the pond, glad to see that Bufo was well and happy.

Bufo said a silent prayer for his friends and was thankful that his best friend was alive and well. They were happy to be back in their homes. Bufo leaped from lily pad to lily pad. Bonzy scooted around, thoroughly enjoying his freedom. He did not want to land up in a cage ever again. They made a pact to be friends forever. They would always help one another and their friends. They both felt sorry for the little girl but they enjoyed their freedom more.

LL apologized many times to Bufo. Bufo accepted his apology and decided to forget the whole episode with LL. LL wanted to be their friend and Bufo said he would forgive him and give him another chance. Bonzy wondered why LL said *'sorry'* to Bufo many times. However, Bonzy did not ask him the reason.

The Blue Birds, Queenie and Danny were busy happily flying amongst the trees. Dizzy was enjoying the nectar of the flowers around the pond. The fishes were happy and content. Even Long Legs had a smile on his face now that Bufo had decided to forgive him. Bufo preferred not to tell Bonzy or it would have hurt him. Bufo and Queenie had a secret that they would tell Bonzy one day. They knew Bonzy had a heart of gold and he did not really want to make any one sad. They must keep the secret for now as there was going to be a celebration party in honor of Bonzy's return the next day. Bufo had come to love this new world. He had decided to make the lily pond his new home. He did miss his Mama and Papa and he knew that he must go and visit them soon. Perhaps, Bonzy and some of his other friends would go with him. He did want to see them, and, as well, Indigo, Flame and Striper. They would be glad to hear of his adventures.

In the meantime, he was going to be happy here, daydreaming on the lily pads. The hubbub of the last few days had died down and soon, the lily pond was quiet again. Bonzy and Bufo never went back to the carrot or the lettuce patch. In fact, they never went near the big House again. They were careful when they left their home in search of adventure. Queenie, Danny, Dizzy and the BBs continued to be one big happy family. The fishes were glad that Bufo had decided to stay. They loved to share the pond with him. They all loved and watched out for each other.

Little Bufo had become the unspoken hero of his new world. Everyone called him *'Little Hero'* and they even gave him a crown. Bufo was not puffed up with pride and all this adoration, he was just happy that he was able to save his dear, dear friend, Bonzy. Bufo had many friends now, even one best friend. Bonzy could not have had a better friend. And, the pond family was one big happy Family.

THE END

BUFO'S PUZZLE ONE

	ACROSS		DOWN
1	Name of the Bunny _____	1	Hero of the Book _____
2	Bird that hoots _____	2	Mr. Horn Rim lived in an _____ tree.
3	Name of one of the butterflies _____	3	What do you hear with? _____
4	Who created the world? _____	4	Name of Flame's friend _____
5	Bufo and Bonzy were having _____	5	Danny was a golden _____
7	Another word for cry _____	6	Bufo was hiding from a _____
8	Flower that grows in water _____	7	What gives warmth to the world? _____
9	Bonzy was caught in a _____	9	Sophie ran _____ her father
10	A nest is a bird's _____	10	The newest family at the pond _____

BUFO'S PUZZLE TWO

| 1 | 6 | 9 | 9 | 8 | | 2 | 6 | 1 | 8 |

| 3 | 9 | 0 | 1 | 8 | | 4 | 4 | 5 | 7 |

| 5 | 2 | 3 | 6 | 5 | | 6 | 5 | 5 | 0 |

| 7 | 2 | 9 | 8 | 4 | | 8 | 9 | 3 | 5 |

| 9 | 4 | 1 | 4 | 4 | 7 | | 10 | 6 | 5 | 4 | 4 |

| 11 | 2 | 3 | 4 | 4 | 7 | | 12 | 4 | 5 | 9 | 0 |

USE THE LETTERS UNDER THE NUMBERS TO SOLVE THE PUZZLE

1	2	3	4	5	6	7	8	9	0
A	B	C	D	E	F	G	H	I	J
K	L	M	N	O	P	Q	R	S	T
	U	V	W	X	Y	Z			

ALL ACROSS

1	Bufo's friend who swims is a _____	2	Bufo was _____ from home
3	It twinkles in the sky _____	4	Man's best friend is a _____
5	Hero of the story _____	6	In the rain, you get _____
7	A parrot is a _____	8	Water freezes to _____
9	Name of the Finch _____	10	Bufo lived in a _____
11	Bonzy is also called a _____	12	A bird lives in a _____

BUFO'S PUZZLE THREE

B	U	F	O	S	M	A	P	L	E
U	T	R	I	L	L	O	W	L	T
T	I	H	V	K	R	O	T	S	R
T	Q	U	E	E	N	I	E	T	E
E	U	C	A	G	E	N	A	M	E
R	E	B	M	A	I	D	P	A	S
F	T	F	O	K	P	I	L	U	R
L	R	E	S	O	O	G	T	N	A
Y	A	Y	L	J	B	O	N	Z	Y
A	W	E	A	C	L	O	U	D	S

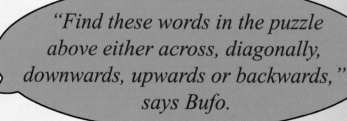

"Find these words in the puzzle above either across, diagonally, downwards, upwards or backwards," says Bufo.

Maple, Bufo, Butterfly, Maid, Ant, Clouds, Goose, Cage, Lotus, Name, Queenie, Bonzy, Trees, Owl, Trill, Stork, Wart, Also, Eye, Rays

Here are the answers to my puzzles

BUFO'S PUZZLE ONE

ACROSS
1. BONZY
2. OWL
3. FLAME
4. GOD
5. FUN
7. SOB
8. LOTUS
9. NET
10. HOME

DOWN
1. BUFO
2. OAK
3. EARS
4. INDIGO
5. FINCH
6. GOOSE
7. SUN
9. TO
10. BB

BUFO'S PUZZLE TWO

ACROSS

1 FISH	2 FAR
3 STAR	4 DOG
5 BUFO	6 WET
7 BIRD	8 ICE
9 DANNY	10 POND
11 BUNNY	12 NEST

BUFO'S PUZZLE THREE

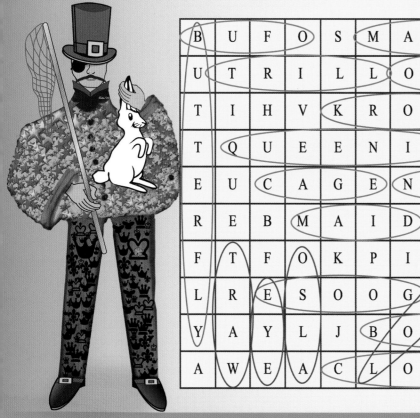

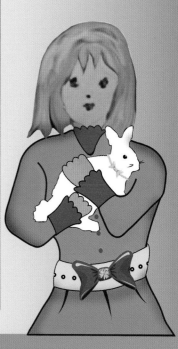

B	U	F	O	S	M	A	P	L	E
U	T	R	I	L	L	O	W	L	T
T	I	H	V	K	R	O	T	S	R
T	Q	U	E	E	N	I	E	T	E
E	U	C	A	G	E	N	A	M	E
R	E	B	M	A	I	D	P	A	S
F	T	F	O	K	P	I	L	U	R
L	R	E	S	O	O	G	T	N	A
Y	A	Y	L	J	B	O	N	Z	Y
A	W	E	A	C	L	O	U	D	S

Acknowledgments

I would like to thank everyone who has supported, inspired and helped me with this book.

Thank you for your honest opinion, which resulted in this wonderful children's book. Thank you to my family who bore the 'highs and lows' as I stumbled through the electronic wizardry to bring this 'Labor of Love' to fruition.

It was pure pleasure to see the book completed, printed, bound and ready for ALL THE CHILDREN OF THE WORLD. Thank you to all who helped BUFO make that very special jump.

TC

All photographs, graphics and sketches are the sole property of NPP, ™ LLC

NATURESDANCE
NPP
PUBLISHING & PHOTOGRAPHIX, LLC ®